Max's Christmas

ROSEMARY WELLS

COLLINS

For Beezoo Wells

William Collins Sons & Co Ltd
London · Glasgow · Sydney · Auckland
Toronto · Johannesburg

First published by Dial Books For Young Readers, New York
First published in Great Britain in 1986
by William Collins Sons & Co Ltd, London
Copyright © 1986 by Rosemary Wells
ISBN 0 00 195328 1

Printed and bound in Hong Kong
by South China Printing Co.

Guess what, Max!
said Max's sister Ruby.
What? said Max.

It's Christmas Eve, Max, said Ruby,
and you know who's coming!
Who? said Max.

Santa Claus is coming,
that's who, said Ruby.
When? said Max.

Tonight, Max, he's coming tonight!
said Ruby.
Where? said Max.
Spit, Max, said Ruby.

Santa Claus is coming right down
our chimney into our living room,
said Ruby.
How? said Max.

That's enough questions, Max.

You have to go to sleep fast,
before Santa Claus comes, said Ruby.

But Max wanted to stay up
to see Santa Claus.
No, Max, said Ruby.

Nobody ever sees Santa Claus.
Why? said Max.
BECAUSE! said Ruby.

But Max didn't believe a word
Ruby said.

So he sneaked downstairs…

and waited for Santa Claus.

Max waited a long time.

Suddenly, ZOOM! Santa
jumped down the chimney
into the living room.

Don't look, Max! said Santa Claus.
Why? said Max.
Because, said Santa Claus,
nobody is supposed to see me!

Why? said Max.
Because everyone is supposed to be asleep in bed, said Santa Claus.

But Max peeked at Santa anyway.
Guess what, Max! said Santa Claus.
What? said Max.

It's time for me to go away
and you to go to sleep,
said Santa Claus.
Why? said Max.

BECAUSE! said Santa Claus.

Ruby came downstairs.
What happened, Max? asked Ruby.
Who were you talking to?
Where did you get that hat?

Max! Why is your blanket
so humpy and bulgy?

BECAUSE! said Max.